Rrra-ah

Rrra-ah

STORY AND PICTURES
BY EROS KEITH

BRADBURY PRESS,
ENGLEWOOD CLIFFS, NEW JERSEY

Library of Congress Number: 78-93086. Manufactured in the United States of America.
First printing   13-783456-X

The text of this book is set in 14pt. Century Expanded. The illustrations are watercolor
paintings reproduced in full color.

For Edith Niblo

Rrra-ah was in his favorite place, on top of a big white clover.
He could see everything, the trees and flowers,
and the pond where he was born.

As he lifted his head, he could feel the summer breeze.

Rrra-ah stuck his nose into a pink clover, closed his eyes and took a deep breath.

He opened his eyes—and it was dark! Rrra-ah trembled.
The sun has fallen, he thought.
Then he heard voices calling—
"Look over here! I've got one!"
And Rrra-ah knew what had happened.
The sun hadn't fallen. . . . He had been caught!

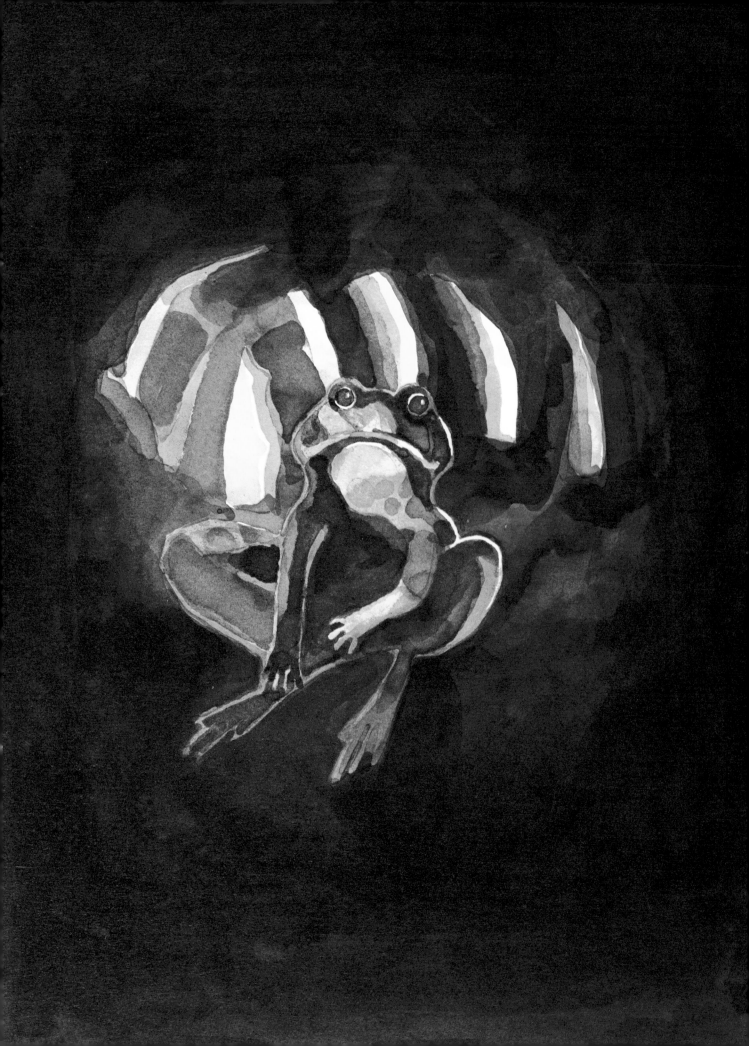

Rrra-ah saw three children!

Boak! How big and ugly they are! he thought.

"Ugh! Is he ugly!" said one of the boys.

"I think he's cute," said the girl.

"He's just a baby. He'll get uglier," the other boy said.

It was a long way from Rrra-ah's meadow
to the children's house. He had been dumped into a big
glass jar. Rrra-ah sat very still
and watched his pond get smaller and smaller.

"Do you think Mother will let you keep him?"

I hope not! thought Rrra-ah.

"What are you going to call him?"

Rrra-ah called his name as loud as he could.

"Frog—just Frog," said the boy with the jar.

Frog! I'm not a frog! thought Rrra-ah.

I'm a toad and my name is Rrra-ah.

"Mother, look! We found a frog!"
Rrra-ah! Rrra-ah! croaked Rrra-ah.

"Well, you didn't find him in the bathtub," said Mother.
"You'll have to find another place to keep him."

Oh, no! thought Rrra-ah. *They are going to keep me!*
One boy brought a box.
One boy brought some grass.
And the girl brought Rrra-ah turtle food.

Rrra-ah didn't like the box or the turtle food.
He didn't eat. He didn't sleep.
I'm not a frog, he kept thinking. *And I'm not a turtle either!*

In the morning one boy said, "Frog, are you ready
to play games with us?"
I'm ready to play escape, thought Rrra-ah,
and he leaped from the boy's hands.

He crashed through the living room, the dining room, the hall . . .

. . . and tipped over three lamps and a vase full of flowers.
But he didn't escape! The children caught him.

That night Rrra-ah was very hungry and sad.
He heard moths at the window and crickets in the grass.
But he couldn't hear the toads by his pond. It was too far away.
He didn't sleep because he was thinking about escaping.

The next day Rrra-ah played the escape game again.
"Stop him!" cried Mother. "He's headed for the kitchen!"

SPLAT!
"That does it!" said Mother. "This house is a shambles."
"That frog has got to go!"
At last! thought Rrra-ah.

The children carried Rrra-ah back to his meadow.
"This is goodbye, Frog," one boy said.

"We'll miss your games," said the other.
"Maybe we'll see you next summer," said the girl.
   Oh, no you won't! thought Rrra-ah—and he was gone.

Then he could see it! His favorite place!

He jumped up and there were the trees and the flowers,
and the pond where he was born.

Rrra-ah stuck his nose into his pink clover, closed his eyes
and took a deep breath.

The sun went down behind the trees and from the pond
he heard other voices calling: *Rrra-ah. Rrra-ah.*